THE BADGER'S BATH

NICK BUTTERWORTH

Collins

An Imprint of HarperCollins*Publishers*

The badger had been doing what badgers do best. Digging. He'd had a lovely day and, as usual when he'd had a lovely day, he was filthy dirty.

"I'm very sorry," said Percy the park keeper, "but you can't come to tea like that."

The badger looked disappointed.

"You'll just have to have a bath," said Percy.

The badger looked even more disappointed.

First, Percy filled a tin bath with warm soapy water. Then he brought out all the things that he liked to use himself when he had a bath. Soap, a loofah, his backbrush, a sponge, some shampoo and, of course, his rubber duck.

The badger sniffed at the soapy water. He didn't like it. He didn't like it at all.

P ercy thought for a moment. Then he
  disappeared and came back with a
jug which he used for wetting his hair
and a shower cap which he used for not
wetting it.

"There. I think that's everything," said Percy. He turned to the badger. "Now, all we need. . ." But the badger was nowhere to be seen.

"Hmm. . ." said Percy. "Now all we need is the badger."

The badger was hiding. He didn't want a bath.

Percy searched and searched but he couldn't find the badger anywhere. He was getting very hot and bothered.

"I really can't understand it," he said. "I always enjoy a bath myself."

P ercy sighed as he looked at the bath full of soapy water. Then he had an idea. He went into his hut.

When Percy came out again he was
wearing his swimming trunks.

"Well, why not?" he said to himself.
He chuckled as he stepped out of his
boots and into the bath.

P ercy lay back in the warm water and
gazed up through the overhanging
branches of a tree.

"Silly old badger," thought Percy.
"I wonder where he's hiding."

There was a sudden rustling above
his head and something black and white
moved amongst the leaves. A strange
idea came into Percy's mind.

"No. . . surely not?" he said to himself.
"Badgers don't climb trees. It must have
been a magpie."

The rustling noise came again.

S uddenly, there was a loud CRACK!
With a great howl, a large black and
white animal fell out of the tree, straight
into Percy's bath water. SP-LOOSH!

For a moment, the badger completely disappeared. Then his head popped up through the soap suds, coughing and spluttering.

P ercy was spluttering too, but with laughter.

"I see you changed your mind about having a bath," he chuckled. "I suppose you didn't want to miss your tea!"

"I didn't know badgers climbed trees," said Percy.

"Well," said the badger, "we're better at digging." He sighed. "Could you pass me the loofah, please?"

NICK BUTTERWORTH

Nick Butterworth was born in North
London in 1946 and grew up in a
sweet shop in Essex. He now lives
in Suffolk with his wife Annette
and their two children,
Ben and Amanda.

The inspiration for the Percy the Park Keeper
books came from Nick Butterworth's many walks
through the local park with the family dog, Jake.
The stories have sold nearly two million copies
and are loved by children all around the world.